*More by the Author*

## Poetry, Essays
## & Short Story Collections

Across the Deserts of My Ghosts
Collecting Shadows
Deukollectrum
Hyperborea
Small Events

## Novels

The Nightingale's Stone

## Anthologies

Unnerving (Volumes 1—3)
The Mighty Pen

# Hyperborea

by David Mecklenburg

Blue Forge Press

Port Orchard ✿ Washington

Hyperborea
Copyright 2019, 2022
by David Mecklenburg

First eBook Edition July 2019
First Print Edition July 2019
Second Print Edition July 2022

ISBN 978-1-59092-944-5

For information about film, reprint or other subsidiary rights, contact: blueforgegroup@gmail.com

 Blue Forge Press is the print division of the volunteer-run, federal 501(c)3 nonprofit company, Blue Legacy, founded in 1989 and dedicated to bringing light to the shadows and voice to the silence. We strive to empower storytellers across all walks of life with our four divisions: Blue Forge Press, Blue Forge Films, Blue Forge Gaming, and Blue Forge Records. Find out more at www.MyBlueLegacy.org

Blue Forge Press
7419 Ebbert Drive Southeast
Port Orchard, Washington 98367
blueforgepress@gmail.com
360.550.2071 ph.txt

*to Shannon*

You always understand.

# Table of Contents

# Hyperborea

by David Mecklenburg

# Epigraph

Of the Hyperboreans, nothing is said either by the Scythians or by any of the other dwellers in these regions, unless it be the Isedonians. But in my opinion, even the Issedonians are silent concerning them; otherwise the Scythians would have repeated their statements, as they do those concerning the one-eyed men. Hesiod, however, mentions them and Homer also in the *Epigoni*, if that really be a work of his.

-Herodotus
*Histories, Book IV Chatper 32*

Let us face ourselves. We are Hyperboreans; we know very well how far off we live. 'Neither by land nor by sea will you find the way to the Hyperboreans'—Pindar already knew this about us.

-Friedrich Nietzsche
*The Anti-Christ*

# Hyperborea I

What is the best place to start looking for a place? Where one is? Or the horizon? There are two things I know: one, I am looking for something. Two, the question contained in the looking is vague. It may not be much, but it's where I start.

What is the best place to start looking for a place? Where am I?

The light—and therefore shadow—is diffuse. It is cold, the wind moves over the flat snowfields which stretch to the end of my gaze and thus becomes horizon. The horizon: ironic that I use a definite article for something I can never reach. A horizon somehow sounds better.

Behind me are many women all named Ada. The younger ones run across the fields going this way, that way. Both directions only exist in the perspective of my hindsight.

It didn't occur to me until I was twenty-four that I had no idea where I was. Before then, I had an excellent idea, courtesy of adolescence—that certain time of pink cynicism that dares to think it has figured out the world.

Enough years have passed that I don't find the twenty-four-year-old or the sixteen-year-old laughable. I don't even shake my head anymore, nor patronize myself. There is too much else to see.

# Winter

*Because I cannot walk here with a daughter, I walk here with my younger self.*

"You will learn this tree, this snow, this life become detached—like rattling marbles, qián coins, crow feathers and lost single earrings in the pocket of the seven-year-old girl who lives in a castle made of rough mist and wind bound mortar.

"Because it is January, we look both ways. You visit me here often, but I am worried about you because good things disappear quickly while the bad remains forever. Or at least until we are dead, which is really the same thing?

"There are not 10,000 arrows darkening the day. only thirteen blackbirds fly across the naked sky and suggest the essence of winter. This season is not our Winter. It is Winter—silent Winter, as exquisite as frost-lace.

*"A riddle is not helpful at all."*

"I am sorry, but you will have to grow into it."

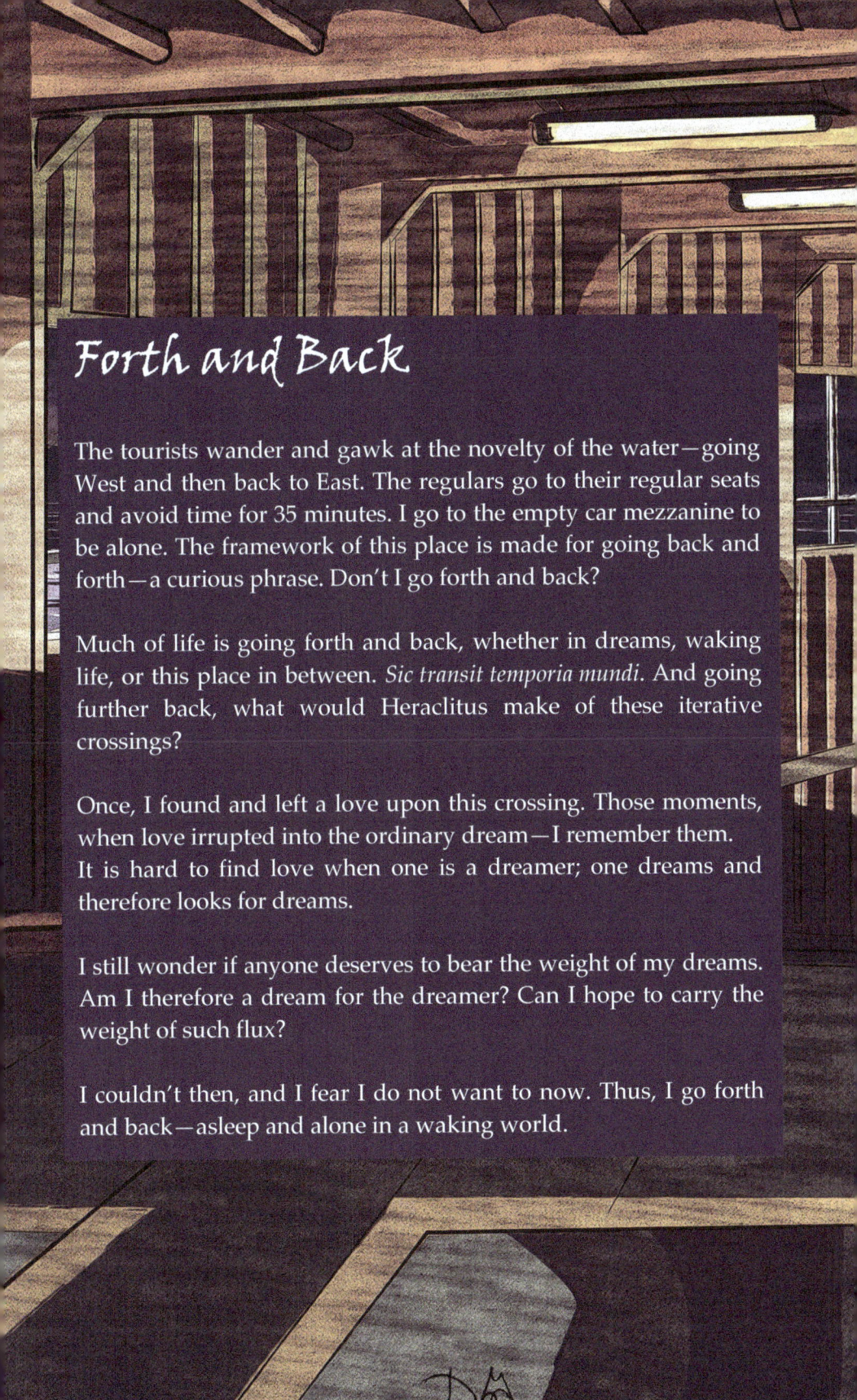

# Forth and Back

The tourists wander and gawk at the novelty of the water—going West and then back to East. The regulars go to their regular seats and avoid time for 35 minutes. I go to the empty car mezzanine to be alone. The framework of this place is made for going back and forth—a curious phrase. Don't I go forth and back?

Much of life is going forth and back, whether in dreams, waking life, or this place in between. *Sic transit temporia mundi.* And going further back, what would Heraclitus make of these iterative crossings?

Once, I found and left a love upon this crossing. Those moments, when love irrupted into the ordinary dream—I remember them. It is hard to find love when one is a dreamer; one dreams and therefore looks for dreams.

I still wonder if anyone deserves to bear the weight of my dreams. Am I therefore a dream for the dreamer? Can I hope to carry the weight of such flux?

I couldn't then, and I fear I do not want to now. Thus, I go forth and back—asleep and alone in a waking world.

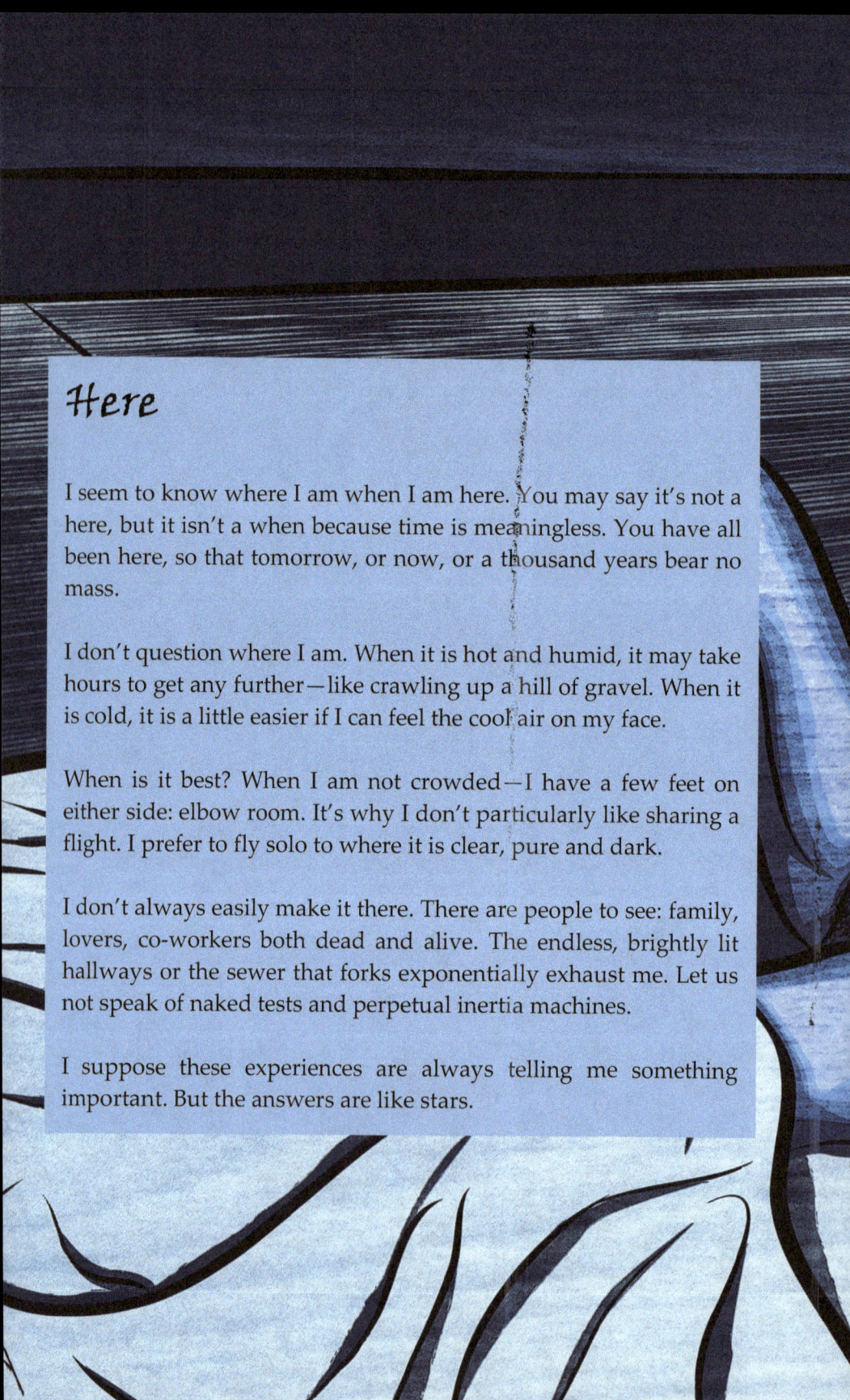

# Here

I seem to know where I am when I am here. You may say it's not a here, but it isn't a when because time is meaningless. You have all been here, so that tomorrow, or now, or a thousand years bear no mass.

I don't question where I am. When it is hot and humid, it may take hours to get any further—like crawling up a hill of gravel. When it is cold, it is a little easier if I can feel the cool air on my face.

When is it best? When I am not crowded—I have a few feet on either side: elbow room. It's why I don't particularly like sharing a flight. I prefer to fly solo to where it is clear, pure and dark.

I don't always easily make it there. There are people to see: family, lovers, co-workers both dead and alive. The endless, brightly lit hallways or the sewer that forks exponentially exhaust me. Let us not speak of naked tests and perpetual inertia machines.

I suppose these experiences are always telling me something important. But the answers are like stars.

# Without You

I don't know why I come here. I guess it's habit. I went for a walk because it's summer and the weather is beautiful. And this is a park. You're supposed to go to a park with weather like this.

All the places we used to go remain the same even though they're changing every day. The people who knew us when we were together are polite enough to not ask me why I am alone. It's written on my face.

But you know the worst place is our home. You were always there when I came back. I was beautiful, and you loved me, no matter whether I was cross, sick, soaking wet, or simply sad. In the kitchen, or on the couch, the sight of you would not leave the corner of my eye. I moved to an apartment with carpet because I could not bear the silence of hardwood floors.

I won't ever forget you. Enough that my body carries me here even when you aren't with me anymore.

I don't know why I bring memories of you with me. I must look strange—as though I've lost you. But I'm the one who is lost.

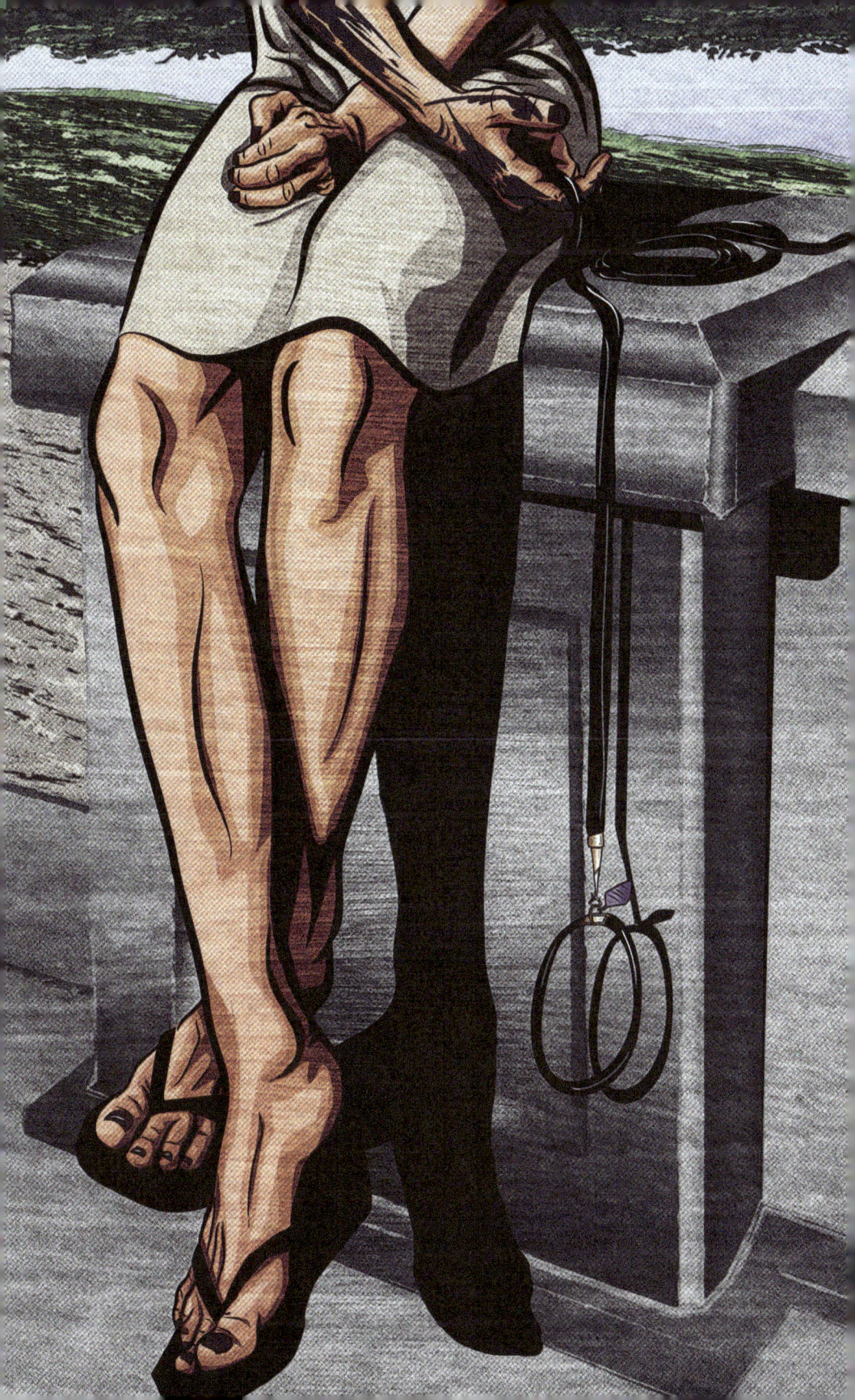

# The Top

When I was a girl, I had faith in a red top that looked like a beet. In that time, the Earth was flat and did not extend beyond the end of my street. As I grew, the horizon of the world grew—an ever widening circle—until the Earth bent in upon itself and so became a sphere.

The Earth also spins upon its axis, whether you see it from the vast perspective of space or the simpler one of a globe—a graduation from the flat place mat inviting you across Mercator's projection of lumpy northern lands and vast Antarctica.

In time, gyroscopic toys became a moving point of contemplation—always in circles. I learned that a compass can both draw a circle and point the way north. Rulers suggested a straight way across the blank page.

I have found that the actual topography has changed the ground I had to cover, riparian distorions and cartographic revisions. Or did they? No, I was altered as the world alters and that is the way it has always been.

At some point, I lost my faith in instruments and maps. I still use them and enjoy their functional beauty. There is a part of me that will always long for the truth they promise. Like an atheist, I still desire that in which I do not believe.

The red top may be the truest guide as it spins in a seemingly random course it does not understand.

# Dissonance, Resolution

In tonal music systems, time and sound often move a circular repetition. The key defines the chords and they move back and forth, perhaps telling some story or merely living through their relationships.

A dissonance changes things. The composer may place one there for dramatic effect: to create a sense of longing perhaps, or general unease—wrath moving into the minor key of self-recrimination. The notes move in time—sometimes slowly, sometimes quickly— until they resolve at the end.

So on that ordinary trip to return your car...

...you were nice enough to let me borrow it. You said you were busy with a project in Winslow and didn't need it for the weekend. I could come and pick you up on Sunday night. I came over early to surprise you. But in driving on the boat, I found the dissonance buried where I could find it and I wondered: was she the composer for placing her compact in your car? Or were you the conductor who left it in?

Regardless, by the end I was resolved.

# Spring

The sakuras were blooming, and it was spring. *The landscape was pregnant with meaning.* I remember thinking that phrase. It was morning, so the park was deserted save for me and a man. I remembered wondering if he could impregnate the landscape. He had dropped his pants and was fucking a hole in the ground. I don't think he knew or cared if I was there or not.

I knew that his semen would decompose, rot, disappear. It would not impregnate the earth. If the man stuck his penis into me, his semen would do much the same.

Because I had become a barren landscape.

I am not a landscape although I am barren. I am not reconstructed. I am not in recovery. The healing has not begun. It is over.

I cannot have children.

> *If I hadn't fucked that guy four years ago. If I had made him wear a condom, or something. If I had gone to the OBGYN when I smelled the pus because we were on the road trip and we didn't bathe except when we swam in that river and we fucked a lot so I just thought it was the smell of all that. Nothing had hurt and I drove the suspicions away; because I was vain; because I was human; because I didn't want to think about it. I was free. I had been on the pill.*

I often had those thoughts once. Less so now.

When I reach menopause then I think I will join some monotheistic religion that I may blame God for giving me the venereal disease we call life, because I will be sterile just like all the other women my age.

What is the difference?

But the sakuras around me suggest a different path. They offer camaraderie and comfort; we are ornamental, ephemeral, sterile and together we are never alone.

# Abyss

The days in all that sun were bright and I felt like an aberration—a campfire burning on the beach at noon. All that could be seen was smoke.

I wanted to be alone. I was alone.

A chain of friends of friends ended with the house of a sculptor who wasn't there, but in a way, he was. The architecture and masonry suggested a thousand moods of volume, movement and the frailty of everything that is born to die. What else is sculpture if not the dance of extension and form into the nothing that makes it?

And next door was the abyss, which constantly suggested that the habits of thought and my body were one. At night the moonlight came to make the shadow visible.

To step off into the Abyss framed by cool reflected light—that is what I wanted. Not that I would fall, but neither would I fly.

Beyond, the town did not sleep. Its inhabitants slept, perhaps a few of them made love, or remained awake in perseverations of thought. We live here and yet we point over there. As if those cliff dwellings over there—that we seldom if ever visit—are our actual homes.

*How was I to tell?* I asked myself that often, and began to doubt that I would ever really know the answer. I had no one there to ask, but that absence—like darkness—allowed a freedom.

There was simply the warm night, the moonlight, and the smell of wild fennel and oranges.

The memory reminds me that I was never standing on anything at all.

# Writing

A page is a map. Or it could be. The symbols that fill either do not really look like the things they purport to be—both are projections of thoughts, which do not have sounds, shapes, nor times.
How could I possibly have a voice in such conditions?

Why don't I say *place*? You see, one of the ways to get lost (a paradoxical construction possible only in language) is to not watch where you are going. Not to know the signs. Not to pay attention to the guidebooks, journals, testimonies and memoirs of those who may have travelled through the Wadi before you. Or the steppe. The careless use of metaphor is a dangerous, widespread practice.

Since most people are capable of using language, most people use metaphor.

I thought I could find my voice on the campus map once. As though it were lying next the library under some Rhododendrons. I did not have the luxury of a guide. A guru. A mentor. A teacher. True, some people gave me enough skill in certain classes, like that one Mountaineer's class on avalanches. Useful, lifesaving, but just enough to stay alive: not to really understand a snowfield. The man who I thought would be my guide, wasn't. He was interested in something else. I served as encouragement, though I didn't know it.

Later, now, I feel lucky to have learned the few rudiments of language he left at the campsite.

But the flints and tinder, the old knife, the compass and the map weren't his to begin with. They don't *belong* to anyone. In traversing the page or the slope—we may claim a mayfly ownership over the act. And someone else will return to…

…a blank page that looks exactly like a blank map—like an untouched snowfield.

# Roots in the Sun

All night long, I didn't know what they were saying. Perhaps it was my imagination, which tends to be stronger in the darkness. I listened to the talk until I fell asleep. This is a strangely found joy of travel in foreign lands where one does not know the language.

The wind was strong last night and that was what all the chatter and clatter was about. It is difficult to tell one speaker from the other when they crowd so. The conversation continues in muted tones upon the morning breeze. Always underfoot, it is protean and sometimes it grows overnight so that the view of the sea, the neighbors or the abyss of time is no longer there in the morning. The sibilance of the language is beautiful even though the syntax, diction and grammar are impenetrable.

After a while the words, sentences, typing, and other utterances all sound the same. This is because down below, the metaphors spread diageotropically—not structures but rhizomes. Language does not have to be understandable to be invasive.

Like all languages, I know this tongue is not endemic to this place. Upon a time it drifted, or was taken, or deliberately planted here. And so it is not my language. Is it anyone's?

Using the words of others—I fear it, but really, I have always been using the words of others. I hold onto this one thought. The game of language is like any other—a matter of learning proficiencies unto perhaps the evanescence of mastery. But the deeper fear remains: if no one understands me, am I really speaking?

Perhaps the structure of my own thought and language is hollow and the words disperse in typical dialectic: up and down; sunward and shade-bound; the *ich und Ding an sich*. But then I wonder, does this language make any distinction between the singular and manifold? I remember a copse of poplars I saw in the mountains once. Could those trees ever make the mistake of inflicting the singular upon themselves?

Very well. But it is not only in the grove of language that I am alone, or have some sense of this place that lies beyond the north wind.

# Hyperborea II

Mornings were the perfect time to fly over the Sea of Okhotsk to Kamchatka. I liked the sound of the place when I was little. I knew it was a long way off, but I didn't know where it was until my uncle pointed it out on the map.

Needless to say, the only way to get there is by flying carpet and you must fly east toward the rising sun. Flying West doesn't work. When you clear the ripples on the sea, you are close because the North Wind has stopped. Sadly, there is only room for one person on the carpet. I knew that if I found my father there, he would not be able to return with me.

Yet it did not matter. In all the times I went there, I did not find him.

From the unforgiving grace of mothers, we know that we are always infants in a world that is not good enough for us. Our fathers—in their various attentions and absences also make us aware of this illusion.

I thought that there was a peak there, from which I could see the truth. I could never find the right mountain. But if I close my eyes, I can still go and stand above the clouds and hear the unbearable silences of the world.

# Outside

The Master's words require an inside—
While it is true that a roof provides beneath—
Inside begs at least one wall.

For shear support, the wall becomes a corner
For enclosure, the third wall is added
Perhaps to keep out the weather.

At this point the walls and roof agree—
A fourth wall would make things cozier
For what they are together

By themselves, they never intended that.
Yet the Inside is nothing
But without it? How can there be structure?

The inside was nothing before
The roof cut off nothing from Heaven
And we did not have a word for blue.

And now when we go beyond the walls
We have a name for Outside and Blue
And we confuse Heaven with a roof.

# Wings

The ballistics of sleep have thrown me above the forest. I do not know how long I have been up here, but I realize that I am not going to fall and die.

I soar and drift, as naked as a... kite because I realize there is a thick collar around my neck. It is old, worn. Someone else's collar is on me now. The leather smells faintly of the sea: a mixture of weeds, fish, and what low tide reveals.

There is a long thin chain attached to my collar. It is made of some metal—as light as smoke and as strong as time. The chain descends into the trees

I cannot tell if I have been tethered or tangled there.

Even here, on raven wings above the canopy, I know the difference is important.

# A Window on November

Words cannot be angry, but writing can be. And angry writing has a back and forth way about it.

I wrote the same things over and over. The coffee was over-roasted: acrid posturing as strong and complex. Like you, I drank it anyway, just as I always do in this moving space. The packets of cream, the seat, the crossing which was nearly empty on a drizzling evening. I traveled back and forth in the certainty of betrayal, of disregard.

How much ink I wasted in the back and forth across that page. The lonely, angry writing.

# Melusine

I have Saturday nights to myself now, but then again, I have every night to myself now.

Self-fulfilling prophecies are best insured with promises you know will not be kept. The test is not so much for passing, but failing, as though a teacher would be free if the student couldn't recite *The Raven*.

In this case it was easy. There was no secret name he had to discover. No quantity of physical abuse. *Just leave me alone one day. Let me have it to myself.*

The week at work exhausted me. For him, it was like cocaine. I thought he would appreciate Saturdays to himself. To spend it with his friends and the interests we did not share. But I learned that things given are really taken by those who wish to own. My time was considered a thing for him to own, amongst other things.

And for a promise I knew he would break, I gave it to him. He did not fail me, and the last fight was frightful. I screamed and broke things. Mine. His. I was no longer myself but a monster he had created by violating Saturday.

I can lay in the tub and unwind by myself now.

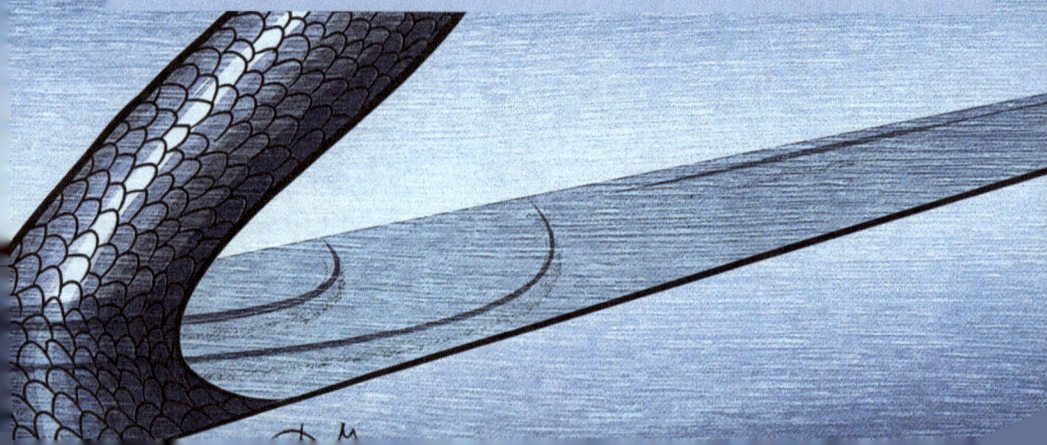

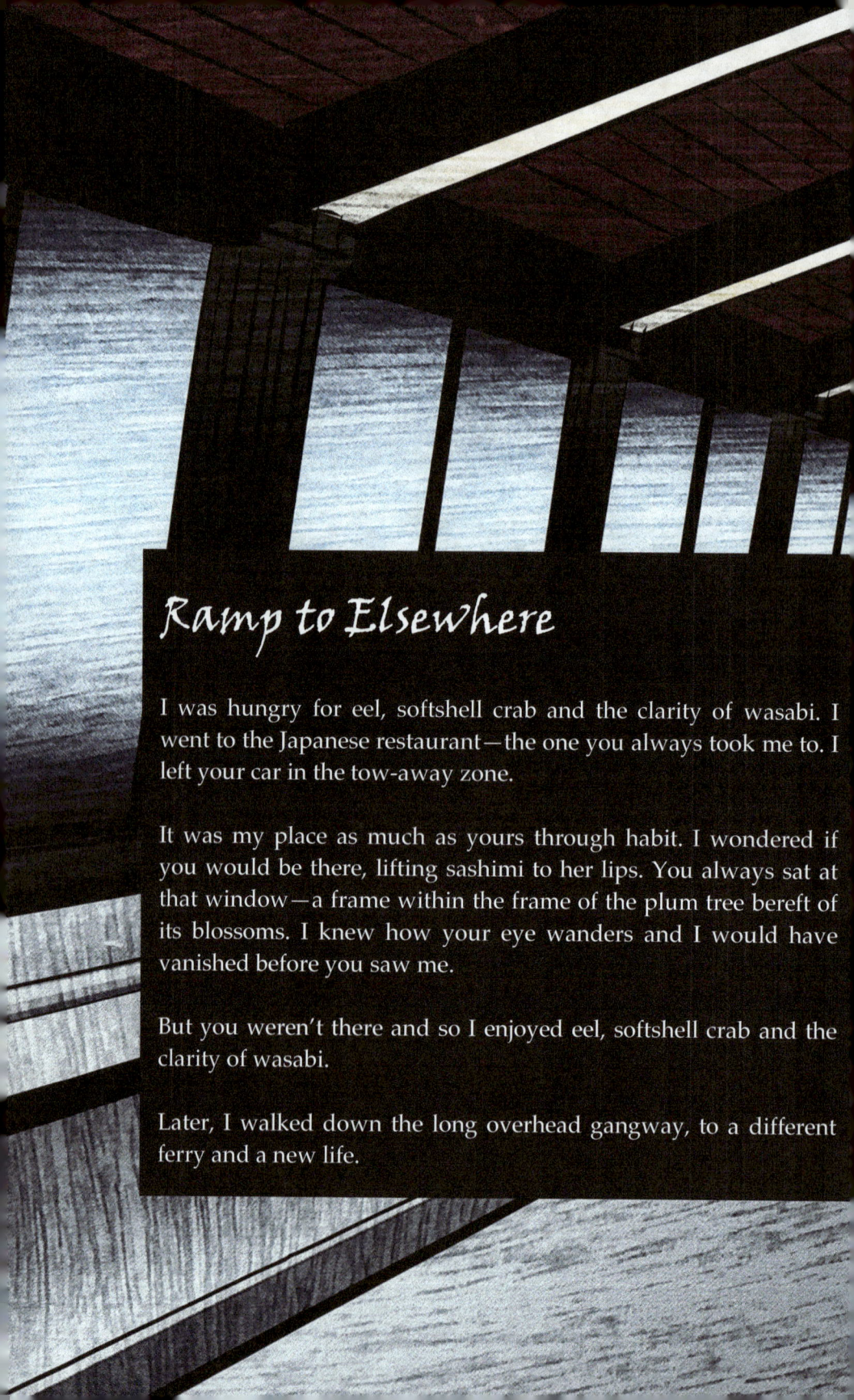

# Ramp to Elsewhere

I was hungry for eel, softshell crab and the clarity of wasabi. I went to the Japanese restaurant—the one you always took me to. I left your car in the tow-away zone.

It was my place as much as yours through habit. I wondered if you would be there, lifting sashimi to her lips. You always sat at that window—a frame within the frame of the plum tree bereft of its blossoms. I knew how your eye wanders and I would have vanished before you saw me.

But you weren't there and so I enjoyed eel, softshell crab and the clarity of wasabi.

Later, I walked down the long overhead gangway, to a different ferry and a new life.

# Mountains

The only truth is mutability—a safe paradox to espouse there. Such thoughts were easy to come by at night by the lake. Speak now, Wild. It is a place where there are no others save those of us in the dark.

I went alone to that lake. "To find myself" is what I told people, but it was really to place the mountains between myself and the vague lands and languages of the human heart. By the lake, I could see the sky for what it was. And was not.

Terror and dread must live in any meaningful ritual. The terror of going alone into the Wild for the women who undertake it is that we may die at any time. Will it be the bear who will snap my bones and easily carve off what flesh I have? Or the angry twisted man who rapes in protracted mutilation? One is an act of digestion, the other, execution. For us, it is wondering how long it will take to die.

I looked at the stars and thought how strange it was that their light, which came from engines long dead, would shine upon my dead body. The silence of the lake and woods assured me that it would not be that night. The moon glittered in hieroglyphs upon the water—a scripture of awe and wonder.

*These stars are only dead if you believe in Time, which here—for a moment—isn't.*

I knew that the bear, the rapist and the lands beyond had returned to their chambers, for I had been here many times before, which is to say, the same time. I gave my best eternal smile to the moon that night. No one could take this away from me, because I did not own it.

Without Time, I did not need to.

# *Fall*

The fall was a time of promise, although I didn't know it then. I couldn't pay attention to it. There was always a rush to the next seminar, an appointment with an undergrad, the part-time job with shifting hours. And then there were the parties.

I was a tall and open secret at the faculty club. I held a gimlet in one hand and his... almost in the other. We came separately, but often left together. I made him look good and was young enough to be his daughter.

On weekends, his real daughter would be at soccer with her mother and he would be at work. Ostensibly.

If work was being in my studio on Capitol Hill going down on me after a bottle of Côte du Rhone. After sex, we'd lie together and talk of Li Bai and Du Fu until he had to go. *My Education* I called it. It was.

It went on until I got too bold and he was too proud of himself. The department chair and a rich alumnus walked in when we were fucking on that old grey couch in his office. The alumnus knew his wife—and was rich, did I mention that? That was the important part.

I disappeared after that. My teaching assistant position and its stipend abruptly ended. They practically shoved my degree under the door, but it felt like they left it on the nightstand. He was tenured, published, and famous. Unscathed.

I continued to read him for a while: searching for myself as some 'creative praxis.' But I was gone.

The fall is a time of promise now. Having been kicked out of a cloistered life, I went into the world—to find this place, I like to think. Far away from halls and hurry, I can savor the chill coming on the air. I sit alone in the afternoon for red, yellow and orange.

# Couture

"Watch what you say."

An absurd statement when you think about it, since the sounds coming out of my mouth are invisible. No, that is a literal, almost scientific approach. But why "watch?" Why not "listen?"

Perhaps watch is more immediate. Perhaps there is a notion that words affect one's appearance.

Words do not lie. People lie. They conceal. They reveal, each according to the game of the moment.

Will this phrase make me look pompous? Overcompensating? Would erudition be best presented with brief, terse statements?

Terse is unnecessary. "Less is more." Van Der Rohe could have said it about so many things.

But how would the world know me, were it not for the layers of words that shape, tuck, and inflate me to the world. And would the world even know me without them?

# Telepathy

"I can read your mind, baby."

"How can you read my mind? That suggests a text—a linguistic text. If you don't actually speak the language of someone, then you cannot read that person's mind. What am I thinking right now?" *Quo usque tandem?*

He does not translate but says: "you know what I mean."

"Oh, you don't speak Latin? Or do you mean a sort of emotional sympathy, like married couples and very old friends? Varieties of inductive familiarity. I barely know you."

"You're overthinking this. Look, when a man and a woman have a connection, it's like your body language. It makes up 80% of what you say. And your body was saying a lot just a bit ago."

"I don't know if you're telepathic, but I can guess you've been to a communication seminar lately. Anyway, all of this presupposes a True Self that the right psychic skills can discover."

"You don't think you have a true self?" He traced the shape of my shoulder blade on my skin.

"I certainly can't say I know it. 'I am large, I contain multitudes.'"

"Is that Nietzsche? I always liked him." He said the name so it rhymed with peachy. I lay on my stomach and thought about peaches. About his balls. About magic. He believed that we could somehow 'communicate with others' without these damn words getting in the way. Or did he? Really? He said nothing. While audiences remain silent, no magic can be sustained forever.

The dinner at Ponti, the walk around Highland Park to look at the view, the drink he bought me were a well-rehearsed series of brief routines. The sex had been good and he actually listened at times. He was a six-hour lie.

He lay down and his breathing softened to that of a sleeping man. There was comfort in that, and I wondered about telepathy some more. Another lie that works because so many of us wish for it to be true.

# Proactivity

I often lie in keystrokes. It's how I learned.

When I started typing, there was a Platonic Form of typewriter. It was a Corona No. 3: the kind Isak Dinesen used. I was too clumsy, too unmusical for the higher form of keyboard. But I could type faster than anyone in my class. Typewriters reminded me of sewing machines. Stolid, metal devices that women used when they worked. They went out of general use. Out of fashion. Times and keyboards change. I still prefer an IBM clickety-clacker: the Model M.

But one day, I paused in my typing when I wrote out my boss's program update declaring that the "unit would engage consumers in dialogue about product suitability and deliverable quality." That these customers were women seeking domestic violence relief made the sentence all the worse. We did not even provide the services but contracted out the work.

How many other secretaries, clerks or whatever we are called, have written a similar sentence on clay, skin, paper or ones-and-zeroes? Does the AI slave wince at such dissimulation through dictation?

Some words I hated, some loved. I cannot remember when I last typed *proactive* save in this elegy. I admit that I still grieve for *hegemony*. Perhaps like all fashionable lies, they are awaiting recycling from their crumpled deaths.

The cursor bears the message: the words may change, but the ribbon and ink remain the same.

# Only Child

I try to imagine what it would be like to have a sister. Maybe we would go to the Balearic Islands to get away. To bitch about our mother. To have that deeply shared story that no longer even needs dialogue until after the second bottle of wine.

I have tried to meet my brother: he is a firefighter and very down-to-earth. But that's as far as I can get. My sister and brother are less real in my imagination than a troll with a horse's head and prehensile hair.

We Only Children are famous for our walls. One of my favorite writers climbs down inside a circular wall called a well. We do not build our walls. We are born behind well-made walls. And then in the magical inverse of this world, it's easier to improve it by doing nothing.

But there is no great danger in looking over the wall. I know I'll never quite fit in. You all may watch the sun set, but I like to see it cast those purple shadows of night on the East. That too is part of a sunset.

# Talos

*Travel to the homes of forgotten gods is a fact of life here.*

You were here when they came with their golden sheepskin—a souvenir of theft and therefore highly valued. And here you remain.

And what else is there to do when they enchant you and remove the nail from your ankle? Though most of your ichor has run out upon the Earth, there is enough pooled in your skull that you may stand and contemplate endurance.

There is only you. You wonder if your purpose was what drained out. You still keep your patina, the favored sister of rust: what else is memory for?

Perhaps if you had not bathed yourself in fire. You destroyed those you embraced or drove them off in terror. Perhaps things would be different.

Yet the vista of the cliffs and the sea remains beautiful, for you are there to bestow that fragile, brazen gift. Do you know that their defeat of you did not unmake you as a god? It was only the unconsidered compunction, the drug called duty that was this long death.

You took the cup even when you said there was no choice. Yet you still believed that it would make things different. You different. And that regret, learned too late, like all regrets, still haunts this holy, forgotten land.

# Nightswimming

My daylit mind had no place for purifying clichés and so I lost myself in the refuse and old dreams of antiquity: marble, terra cotta the mosaics of dolphins, octopuses and women—swimming.

The ochre day gave way to sapphire and that was when I went to the pool and swam each night as though it were my last. In that well-locked place I was alone and certain that one last swim would make me clean.

In that fleeting, eternal summer I can forget the memories of nows and the updates to hindsight that are as clear as they were then. The question remains in the past because I put it there, History is ripples on the blue tiles.

I do not sleep-swim. What is consciousness if it swims bereft of thens and laters? Dream. In any pool, at night, alone, is not this water all water? How can I break it into nights and laps?

*In.*

My right arm curls through the water, a drag of bubbles and the sky gives my hair a glossy blackness. The edge occurs—a somersault and push—counted and forgotten.

A woman becomes the water and the water becomes a woman. In this liquid sovereignty, I may still blend the definite and indefinite. This is how I am not a birth, nor death: only being.

Self-contained—a sorcery of self-made prayers and memories—I step in again and say farewell to summer.

For a time.

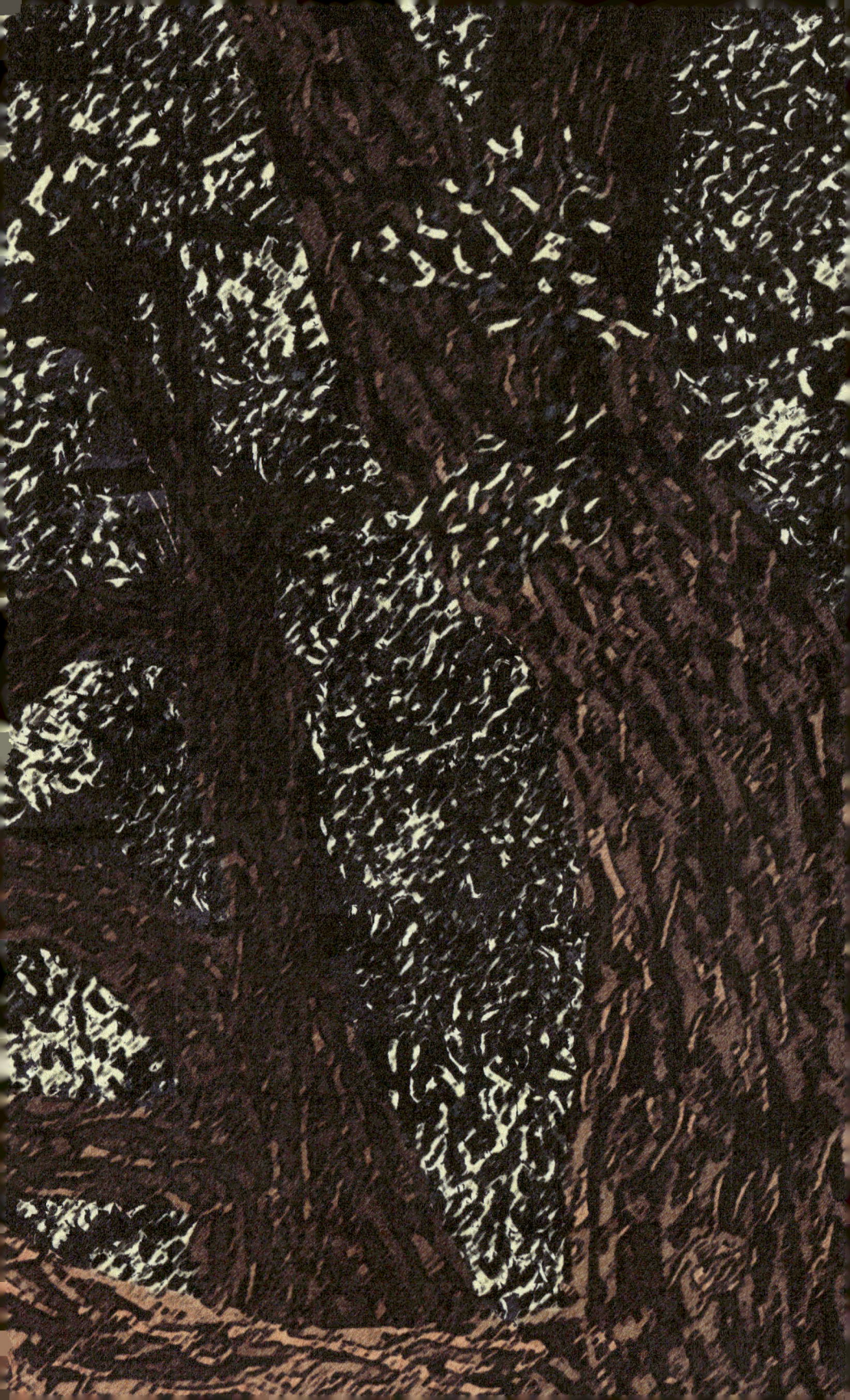

# Fire, Wood

The tree did not move, which meant that it was there every day, and perhaps that is the reason it felt like any day. Without perception, without thinking, they feel very much the same.

But it was not an everyday because of his laughter across the clearing. We were all staying in the old cabin, and I could hear him laughing at some joke. I barely knew him, and so that was the first time I had really heard him laugh. He knew how to use an axe and made short work of the wood for the fire. We talked about salmon—they were his profession: how they swam, how they ate, how they died. Later, we cooked a whole Chinook over that fire and made bread in a dutch oven. The Sancerre was barely cooled by the stream but we didn't care. It was only an appetizer for the stories we all told to one another in the summer night.

Couples drifted off from the group and that night I was not one of the people by the fire.

Like our stories and ourselves, everything has been alive or dead, once.

After we made love, we lay at the end of the reach of the fire's light, and studied the illuminated flowers waiting for day and bees. The briar puffs remained in my hair—seeds for peregrinations of generations into the next valley.

I have saved them, but they remind me of the emptiness in my body that some other man had left. My lover did not know. Neither could I since I did not have the bravery to guess. It was easier then, to watch the summer stars and feel his back. Freedom meant him and hope: not the awkward comfort of solitude.

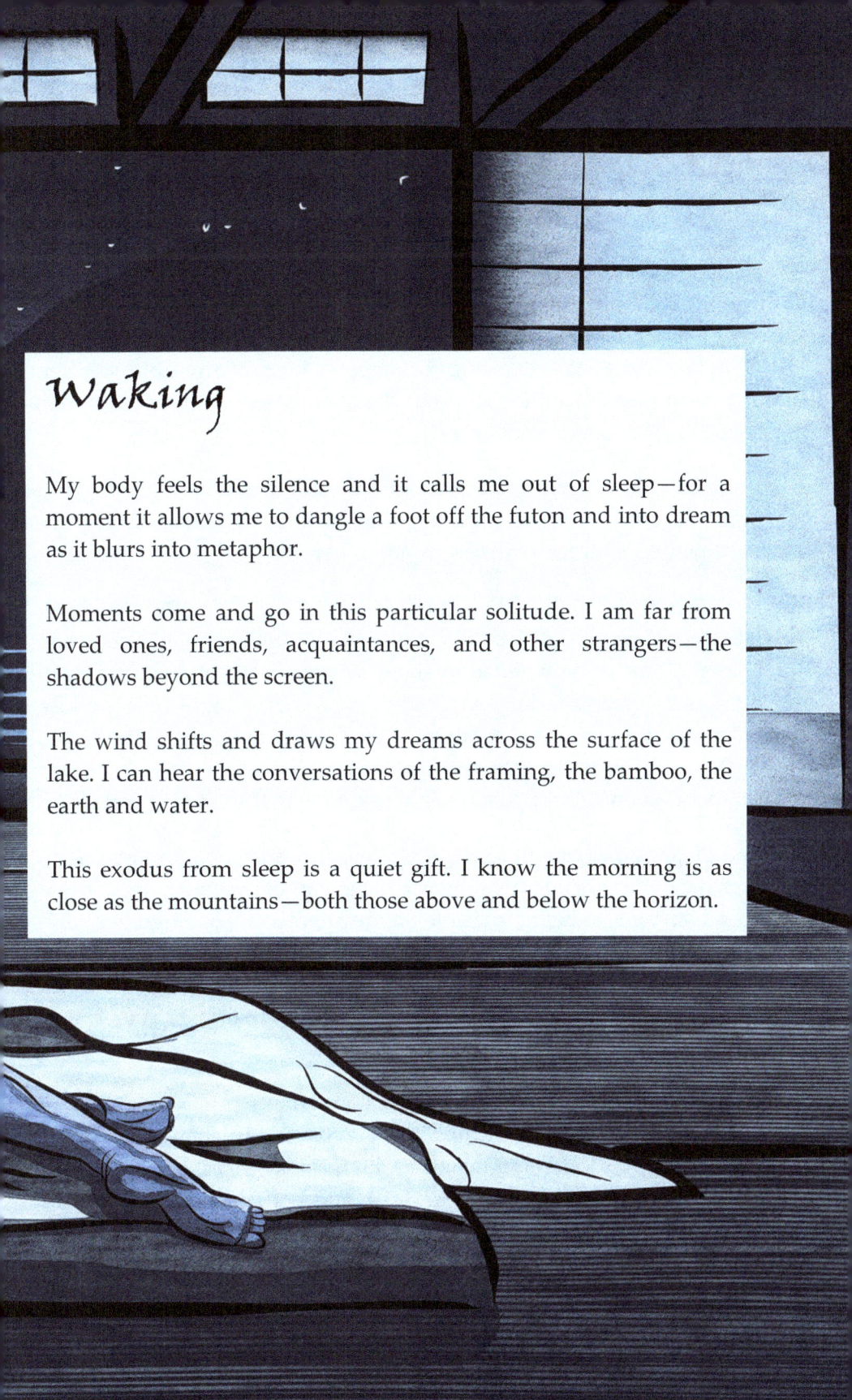

# Waking

My body feels the silence and it calls me out of sleep—for a moment it allows me to dangle a foot off the futon and into dream as it blurs into metaphor.

Moments come and go in this particular solitude. I am far from loved ones, friends, acquaintances, and other strangers—the shadows beyond the screen.

The wind shifts and draws my dreams across the surface of the lake. I can hear the conversations of the framing, the bamboo, the earth and water.

This exodus from sleep is a quiet gift. I know the morning is as close as the mountains—both those above and below the horizon.

# Fading

I remember that they all saw me once, but I have begun to fade. I do not need a ring, I simply became middle aged. The world became oblivious to me, just as I suspect I have been oblivious all these years.

Oblivion is the state of being forgotten, a kind of invisibility: when anyone under 30 cannot see you: the state wherein my clothes give shape to what others cannot see.

I do not mean children. Children can still see elves, ghosts, and unicorns, who are so very old that they have disappeared entirely for most people. Children still see grandmothers.

In reciprocation to the young men who do not see me, I turn them all into the same young man. I was unsure of the male gaze when younger. Part of me wanted to stand before it. Part of me recognized my face… already fading. My breasts were never big—their promise faded early. My ass and legs were nice for a skinny girl, but I'm tall. That made me noticeable and unforgivable to many women. I was competition once, I suppose, even though I was oblivious to that.

I no longer go to bars that require a bouncer and therefore no one to card me or try to slide his finger into the gap between my legs. There are advantages to being invisible. In the afternoon, I shall go to a café-bar. Somewhere I can find a middle-aged waiter or bartender—a man who is handsome and attentive: a grown-up. In our fading, we find camaraderie—that instance where the shadow world is shared and enjoyable.

Today I want a French 75 before lunch. Perhaps a glass of Sancerre with the cold chicken and mayonnaise. Some cornichons. A head of endive with lardons. Barques of dark chocolate bearing mousse and raspberries. A single espresso to finish and perhaps a glass of sherry because I am getting older. I will then ride into oblivion—and a kind of serenity.

# Schweigen

*Have you heard this one?*

*I sat on the edge of the pond and marveled at the water-striders.*
*The wind scattered them like leaves and they remained dry.*
*I knew that I would sink and drown.*

Oh, you're here. Perhaps it's glass not water. Can you hear the grinding, popping fracture lines? It's different than ice. Broken glass cuts. But I'll shift metaphors slightly: let's break the ice…

…that's cooled everything because I wasn't supposed to be here. But I didn't conceal the truth. I just didn't want to see you. Not now.

Please don't be upset. I'm not going to lie. I'm an only child and we don't lie very well. You'd see through it and be insulted.

I like to use words. When I was younger I could gush. Sometimes just for the sound. Sometimes for the complex stew of ideas I hoped would be measured in the depth of feeling. Or brightness of detail. But I learned that no one really wanted to listen to all that. Compression seemed better, at parties or work. Or here.

*I learned it was even better to abridge my words. Elide the Latin and repeat what powerful men say. The silence of the smallest talk came naturally then.*

I consider my text carefully when I turn in front of my three-panel mirror of past, present and future tense. Does this fit right? Will she understand me? Will he get this? Will they even care?

You think I've been avoiding you. You are right. Not all days. Just now I wanted to be alone. To have this coffee and air to myself and my thoughts. But now you know. I have been apprehended. Why?

After a life whereof I cannot speak, sometimes I want to be silent.

# Summer

I am on vacation, which means I have left an emptiness behind where I usually live.

I think of my apartment and how the light shines on a chair in the corner, how the sound of running water is so insistent there. The mauve walls blush a little yellow on Sunday mornings. Is it all still there while I think about it here in the Garden of Philonus and Hylas?

Is it only in my head?

What if I have forgotten where I was? If I look out at the horizon, I become obliterated in the rising sun as all shall be—even the sun itself. Can I say with certainty that I ever existed? Shouldn't there be someone else—the Father of Bishop Berkeley to make me real?

But I'm happy. I am not going to my job on time or at all. I am not eating lunch at 10 minutes after noon and waiting for microwave. This place is warm and I can wear only my plum colored shorts and top in the morning.

The streets are not familiar and I have to think while I count out the coins for the man on the corner selling tamarind water. He winks and I understand that in his language 'gracious lady' retains a measure of dignity for both of us.

Personas, places—spirits in the world? I am older with this sunrise, as I am with all of them and I remain unsure. But when I am on vacation, it doesn't seem to matter—a souvenir of Summer.

# En la Orilla

Yes, it's the same beach where I can go alone, but the subtle work of tide and wind make it different each day. Is it the cerulean of the sea, or the ultramarine of the sky? The blues are so different and yet they make the horizon all the vaster.

There are people out there in ships whom I have met before but never seen. They wait until the night comes to sail in closer to this shore. There is a cat of course. I am not even that fond of cats, but this one is a pleasant mystery unto herself and is neither tyrannical nor obsequious. We leave each other unto ourselves.

The ritual is the same within this place outside my usual rituals. I listen to Chopin while I eat a breakfast of beans, eggs and tortillas. I gather my few things for the beach and then say hello to the concierge. She is writing her memoirs of being a psychic prostitute. She nods. The nod is sufficient.

I oil my skin and am glad I have brought only one book for it removes the aspect of choice. I am not here to choose. I simply want to lie on the beach and read.

At noon, I wonder if I have been here all of my life, which is only this day.

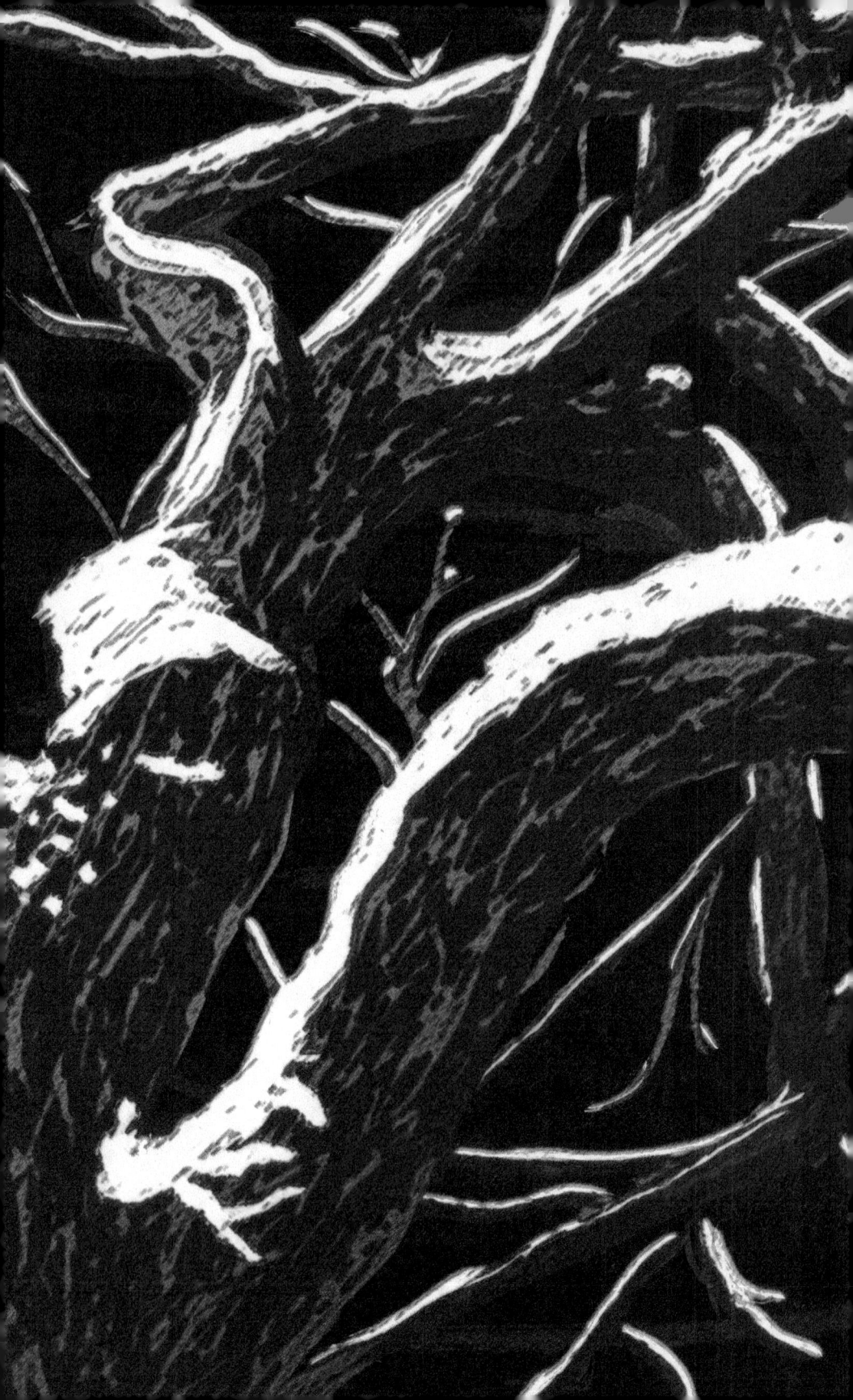

# Snow, Stars

He wasn't there and time had a fire to slowly smother and grey ashes to make out of blackened wood. Alone again, I had put on my snowshoes to get away from my drunk friends who pursued sex or sleep. The snowshoes were loud, crunching invasions and so I did not go far. But it was far enough away from the absence of someone's heart beating against my back: the insistent breath of now in my hair.

The sky was free of clouds and the sun, and time unrolled on the silent snow—Winter: a place and time where I was free to think.

Time out of mind—an everyday phrase for something outside the every of the day. And everydays continue. I looked up at the stars and considered the turn of the world and the time slipping from my mind.

*Why should I consider this one night any different?*

Because it was the longest of the year? Because the Earth had reached a certain point in is ellipse that made it all a trusted calculation of imagination? Would the seeds beneath the snow understand the difference between the Sun turning north again, or the Earth spinning like a listing top on the Solar plane? Were the every of days any different for Ptolemy or Copernicus?

I watched my breath become a ghost in the moonlight and knew that whichever truth I chose, Winter was the best season to step into the land beyond the north wind.

# Sundeck

After you have crossed the Puget Sound, you must disembark. When I first moved here you could remain on the ferry for a round trip, but the complications of telling the world what to do finally came home like a Roman education at the hands of Alaric. We are told it is for security, and I believe it, since safety is a persuasive way to cut people off from one another.

But if it's an inconvenience, it's not unwelcome. I walk off into possible change, even if I am coming back to where I started from. The boat is not merely an ampersand between here and there and the crossing itself changes the here and there. I don't know if he lives over there with her, or another her anymore. It doesn't matter now. Thanks to maritime security measures, I can measure that town as my own here, for a few minutes until it's time to go back on board.

I go up to the sundeck to see the spectacle of outside between two thens: the one in the past and the one in the future. Sometimes, the ferry has crossed between a rock and a hard place. Sometimes it shuttles between the Devil and the Puget Sound, which is also deep and blue.

I go to the sundeck, and there, across the shifting currents is another boat—and someone waves.

The course of the crossing between here and there begins with a single gesture. And I finally feel brave enough to wave back.

# Doing Nothing

The days began, like all solitary vacations, with the saffron yellow of novelty. I slept at odd hours and made a list of things that I would never get to. Discoveries—beautiful, banal, and disappointing—came into the sphere of my experience. I read the novel I had bought for this trip. I saw a museum or two and wondered at the lives of those who created such things.

Prayer consisted of breakfast in a café where the language was not that of home. I was grateful for that and a loaf of bread and marmalade—a communion that made me stop and consider the bitterness pervading the sugar of the world. Each afternoon I came here to watch the sea. At times, the rhythm of the world found some silence in my mind to allow the counterpoint of unique moments to rise in careful notes. I felt each wave was different and the gulls never flew in exactly the same courses.

The sun today and paella tonight are framed by tomorrow. Tomorrow I return home by several means: a taxi, an airplane, the knowledge of what I must do when I have returned and the real uncertainty of everything.

The burdensome blessings of space and time are a framework that I possess and possess me, but in the sun—whose light I have never altogether trusted—I notice shadows once again. Some are sharp and dark, while others reveal the continuum of tonalities that provide the bulk of our lives. Home is a symphony of diffuse gray made up of I don't what is going to happen. It is, for better or worse, inescapable save for a few moments of nothing. But that is why I am here for one more day.

"Doing nothing is hard work." How strange it seems that language, which appears as orderly as the cut stones I sit on is really as arbitrary as the raw rocks waiting in the earth. Does language help in such a place? No: if you are looking for meaning. Yes: if you simply want to enjoy the permutations of its craft and architecture.

And so the summer slips away on this last day—a day where reason and feeling take one last drink together and remain silent while the afternoon races by the sun.

# Hyperborea III

How long have I waited at the rooftop of the world for it to come to me?

Time is both much and little here and time is quiet. There is always a now shifting at the boundary of my sight. I bring it with me wherever I go so that when I walk toward it, it retreats to where it always is. It is the only circle of my life that is constant and mutable, whether I walk in cities, towns, mountains or on this steppe.

Since the world bent in upon itself, the end of the world could be anywhere. This is the tree at the end of the world. The tree is rooted and I wander but we both remain here. We know the water of truth is a fable from the time we were seedlings.

What is the truth? What is any truth but a horizon—which we share. When the snow melts, we shall have enough to drink so I give a smile of winter to the tree.

www.ingramcontent.com/pod-product-compliance
Lightning Source LLC
Chambersburg PA
CBHW060600100726
47907CB00005B/1457